This Boxer Books paperback belongs to

. . . .

www.boxerbooks.com

To Isobel and Alasdair
J.A.

First published in hardback in Great Britain in 2010 by Boxer Books Limited.
First published in paperback in Great Britain in 2011 by Boxer Books Limited.
www.boxerbooks.com

Text and illustrations copyright © 2010 Jonathan Allen

ISBN 978-1-907967-06-1

1 3 5 7 9 10 8 6 4 2

Printed in China

All of our papers are sourced from managed forests and renewable resources.

I'm not Sleepy!

Jonathan Allen

Boxer Books

Baby Owl had stayed up all night
as every owl does.

And he looked very sleepy.

"Bedtime for a sleepy Baby Owl!"
called Mum.

"I'm not sleepy!" grumbled Baby Owl.

But he couldn't help giving
a great BIG s t r e t c h .
Then along bounced
Grey Squirrel.

"Well, you look sleepy to me,
Baby Owl!" said Grey Squirrel.

"I'm not sleepy!"
said Baby Owl.

"I was just stretching my wings," said Baby Owl. "I will be learning to fly soon, you know."

Baby Owl settled back on his perch
and yawned a great BIG yawn.

"That was a VERY big yawn!"
said Mouse. "What a sleepy
Baby Owl you are this morning."

"I'm not sleepy!" said Baby Owl.
"I was just yawning because I am bored.
Owls need lots of excitement, you know."

Baby Owl settled back on his perch. And before long, his head started to nod and his eyelids began to droop.

Then along came Woodpecker.

"WAAA!"
said Baby Owl.

"Oops, sorry!"
said Woodpecker,
"I didn't know there was
a sleepy Baby Owl on the
other side of this tree."

"I am NOT sleepy!"
shouted Baby Owl. "I was thinking.
Owls are very wise, and we spend
lots of time thinking, you know."

Then along came Dad.
"You look VERY sleepy, Baby Owl,"
said Dad. "It's time you were in bed."

"But I'm not sleepy!" cried Baby Owl.
"Everyone keeps telling me that I am,
but I'm not! I'm thinking!"

"I'm thinking too, Baby Owl,"
said Dad, lifting Baby Owl
from his branch.

"And I'm thinking that, sleepy or not,
you are certainly very grumpy.
Come in now and I will read
you a bedtime story."

"All right, Dad,"
said Baby Owl, snuggling
into his dad's soft feathers,
"but make it a nice long
story because I'm not at
all slee . . . "

"Sleepy?" Dad smiled.
Baby Owl was fast asleep.

"Goodnight,
Baby Owl."

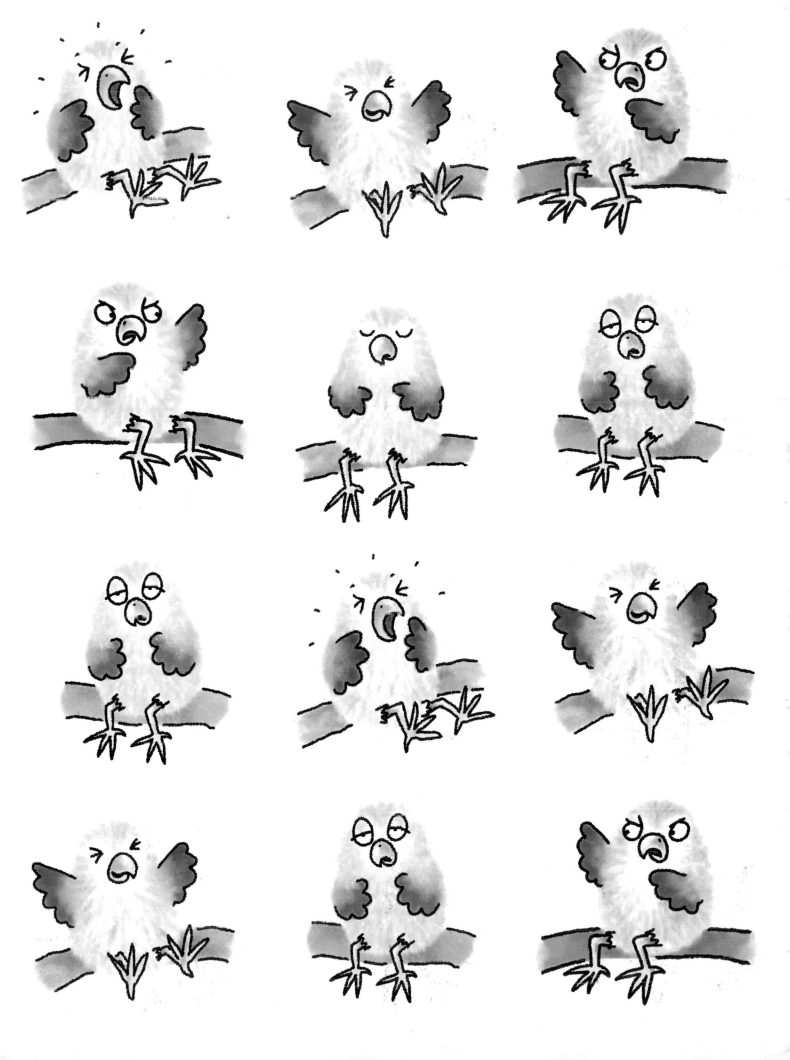

More Baby Owl stories for you to enjoy!

Written and illustrated by Jonathn Allen

'**Absolutely hilarious**'
– *Kirkus*

'**Made me laugh out loud . . . a delight**'
– *The Observer*

"**... the simplest of stories, but one that will bear frequent retellings.**"
- *The Financial Times*

I'm not Cute!
Baby Owl decides to explore the woods, but every animal he meets thinks he is so cute and so fluffy that they want to give him a hug! Baby Owl tells them all "I'm not cute!" A perfect bedtime read that all children will relate to. A real hoot!
ISBN 978-0-954737-39-3

I'm not Scared!
Baby Owl is out for a moonlight stroll through the woods but each animal he bumps into tells him not to be scared! Can Baby Owl convince them that owls are meant to be out at night, and, more importantly, that he is not scared?
ISBN 978-0-954737-39-3

I'm not Santa!
Baby Owl is taking a Christmas Eve stroll through the woods with his sledge, when Baby Hare mistakes him for Santa. "I'm not Santa!" Baby Owl insists, and a comic, snowy Christmas tale unfolds.
ISBN 978-0-954737-39-3